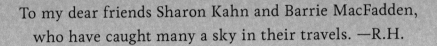

To my dear friends Sharon Kahn and Barrie MacFadden,
who have caught many a sky in their travels. —R.H.

For Duncan, who has been by my side
through both sunny and stormy skies. —E.D.

Text copyright © 2020 by Robert Heidbreder
Illustrations copyright © 2020 by Emily Dove
First published in Canada and the U.S. in 2020, and in the U.K. in 2021 by Greystone Books

20 21 22 23 24 5 4 3 2 1

Greystone Kids / Greystone Books Ltd.
greystonebooks.com

Cataloguing data available from Library and Archives Canada
978-1-77164-631-4 (cloth)
978-1-77164-632-1 (epub)

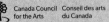

MIX
Paper from
responsible sources
FSC® C016973
FSC
www.fsc.org

Editing by Kallie George
Copy editing by Antonia Banyard
Proofreading by DoEun Kwon
Jacket and interior design by Sara Gillingham Studio
Jacket illustration by Emily Dove
The illustrations in this book were rendered in watercolor, ink, and a tablet.

Printed and bound in China on ancient-forest-friendly paper by 1010 Printing International Ltd.

Greystone Books gratefully acknowledges the Musqueam, Squamish, and Tsleil-Waututh peoples
on whose land our office is located.

Greystone Books thanks the Canada Council for the Arts, the British Columbia Arts Council,
the Province of British Columbia through the Book Publishing Tax Credit,
and the Government of Canada for supporting our publishing activities.

Canadä

Canada Council   Conseil des arts
for the Arts   du Canada

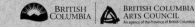

BRITISH
COLUMBIA

BRITISH COLUMBIA
ARTS COUNCIL
An agency of the Province of British Columbia

Robert Heidbreder • ILLUSTRATIONS BY Emily Dove

CATCH
the
SKY

Playful Poems on the Air We Share

GREYSTONE KIDS

GREYSTONE BOOKS • VANCOUVER/BERKELEY

Catch the Sky
Look up! Gaze round!
Cast eyes to air.
Catch the sky
that we all share.

Sunrise
Rosy, red arms
caress the sky,
smiling sun
waving **HI!**

Sunshine
Don't catch its eye!
But hug its power.
Wrap up tight
in sun's light shower.

Sunflower
Sunflower, standing
taller than me,
what do you see
that I can't see?

Honeybee
Sweet honeyed sound,
from flower to flower
buzz-buzzing around
hour to hour!

Dragonfly
A dragon's flying
with dragon-sure flair.
Its gleaming wings
glitter the air.

Butterflies
Orange, black, white
pirouette the sky.
Monarch wings
go dancing by.

Wind
Trees, clouds, birds
all feel it's there.
Invisible wind
rustles the air.

Leaves
Swinging, clinging,
    all sizes and shapes,
    leaves wait for fall
        to make their escapes.

Kites
Diamonds, sleds,
small boxes in air,
kites bound to ground
sky-dive everywhere.

Balloons
Balloon moons
   drifting near,
      a birthday party's
         happening here!

Squirrel

Scurrying,   a squirrel conspires
to balance   on tight power wires.

Starlings

In a line as long   as roads below,
starlings perch,   to watch Earth's show.

Helicopter
Beyond bird's flight
  on through thick cloud
  a chopper mounts,
    proudly loud.

Hot-Air Balloon
A balloon belly floats,
   a bob and a go,
   a hot-air balloon
      on a slow-go show.

Giant Cloud
Downy-filled sky,
   one cloud spread wide,
   a giant's quilt
      for a giant to hide.

Elephant Cloud
White elephant cloud,
strolling the blue,
do you step softly
    all the day through?

Rain
Will it sprinkle,
    drizzle, downpour?
        Ready, dark cloud,
            for a little or . . . MORE!

Storm
Rumbling storm train
thunders the sky.
Off lightning tracks
sparks flash and fly.

Rainbow

Look, they're there!

See them fast-gliding.

Up, down the rainbow

bright elves are sliding.

Paragliding
Paragliders
    slow-float the skies.
A feast of colors
for eager eyes.

Crows

Dark sprays of wings
    through fading light,
crowd-clouds of crows
    head home for the night.

Moonrise
Night beams in.
Up the moon rises.
Catch the sky's
new night surprises.

Fireflies
There—not there—
off—on—switching—
luminous yellow,
fireflies' bewitching.

Bats
Black on black,
swish-soft swirls.
Night bats feast
in whirling twirls.

Shooting Stars
Flashes fast
  as racing cars,
  silent roars
    of shooting stars.

Fireworks
Crackles, boom-bursts,
razzle-dazzle display,
fireworks make night
like the day.

Northern Lights
Pulsing hues
　　charge the nights.
　　High up swirl
　　　　the northern lights.

Snow
Snow flows down,
 buries towns deep,
 flake by white flake,
 in silent sleep.

Good Night, Sky
Draw the curtains.
Into warm beds.
Sky's treasures we shared
will dance in our heads.